Didn't we have a lovely time!

For all the children and teachers who have come to the farm over the last forty years

M.M.

Published 2016 by Walker Books Ltd
87 Vauxhall Walk, London SE11 5HJ

2 4 6 8 10 9 7 5 3 1

This book has been typeset in Goudy Old Style

Printed in China

British Library Cataloguing in Publication Data:
a catalogue record for this book is available from the British Library

ISBN 978-1-4063-7163-5

www.walker.co.uk

Didn't we have a lovely time!

Michael Morpurgo

Quentin Blake

WALKER
BOOKS

It takes six long hours by coach from London down to Devon, and there, in a large Victorian manor house with views over to the hills of distant Dartmoor, we all live together for a week, all forty of us, teachers and children, and we all become farmers. We practically live in our wellies! Every day, from dawn to dusk, we're out working on the farm. We go for long muddy walks, eat three good hot meals a day, sing songs, tell stories around the fire in the evenings, and sleep like logs.

I'm a teacher in London, in the inner city. I've been taking the children down to Nethercott once a year for nearly forty years now. For me and for them it's the week in the year we all look forward to most. I love to see the children working hard and purposefully out on the farm feeding calves, moving sheep (and helping to lamb them too in the spring), making hay in the summer, planting trees in the winter. They groom Hebe the Haflinger horse who everyone loves, muck out stables and sheds, dig potatoes, collect eggs and logs, and pick apples and blackberries too, sometimes. The children do it all, and they love it – mostly, anyway.

The great thing is that we all work alongside real farmers and get to feel like proper farmers. We know that everything we are doing is useful and important to the farm, that our work is appreciated.

Every year after our week in Devon, we come back to school and the whole place is buzzing with excitement. Everyone wants to hear all about it. In the playground and in the staff room, all the stories of our time down on the farm at Nethercott are told again and again. Some are true, some are not so true, maybe a bit exaggerated, but they all make great stories.

There are the magic moments: a calf being born, the glimpse of a fox or a deer in Bluebell Wood, an otter slipping into the water of the River Torridge. And the triumphant moments: moving two hundred sheep all the way down through the village with the children as sheepdogs, and not losing a single one of them – child or sheep!

The rescue of a duck that went walkabout and would have been eaten by the fox if we had not found her before nightfall. It was Ho who carried her home to her shed.

And best of all, there are the little disasters: Mandy's welly being sucked off in the mud, Jemal being chased by the goose, and Miss Tripp, who ran off down the hill, tripping, and ending up rolling over and over down the hill instead. Miss Tripp *tripping*, everyone thought, was the funniest moment of the whole week, and there were lots of them.

There are tragic moments too: the dead crow we found by the gateway, the lamb born too small to survive.

The children always write a lot about the time down at Nethercott, paint pictures of it, make plays of it, and I know they dream about it too, as I do. I am quite sure they never forget it.

But one year, and this was a long time ago now, something so extraordinary happened on one of these visits that I felt I had to write it down, just as it happened, so that I should never forget it, and because I know that in years to come, as memory fades, it is going to be difficult to believe. I've always found miracles hard to believe, and this really was a kind of miracle.

The boys and girls at our school come from every corner of the earth, so we are quite used to children who can speak little or no English. But until Ho joined us, we never had a child who didn't speak at all. He was about seven then; ten now. In the three years he'd been with us, he had never uttered a word. As a result he had very few friends, and spent much of the time on his own.

We would see him sitting by himself, reading. He read and he wrote in correct and fluent English, more fluently than many in his class who'd been born just down the street. He excelled in maths too, but never put his hand up in class, was never able to volunteer an answer or a question. He just put it all down on paper, and it was usually right. None of us ever saw him smile at school, not once. His expression seemed set in stone, fixed in a permanent frown.

By the time of our Nethercott trip, we had all given up trying to get him to talk. Any effort to do so had only one effect – he'd simply run off, out into the playground, or all the way home if he could. Neither the child psychologist nor the speech therapist could ever get a word out of him either. They told us it was best simply to let him be – to do whatever we could to encourage him and give him confidence, without making demands on him to speak. They weren't sure whether Ho was choosing not to speak, or whether he simply couldn't. It was a mystery.

All we knew about Ho was that he was an orphan boy. Ever since he'd arrived in England he'd been living with his adoptive parents and in all that time he hadn't spoken to them either, not a word. We knew from them that Ho was one of the Boat People, that as the long and terrible war in Vietnam was coming to an end he had managed to escape, somehow. We could only imagine what dreadful suffering he must have lived through, the things he had witnessed, how it must have been for him to find himself alone in the world, and in a strange country. There were a lot of Boat People coming to England in those days, mostly via refugee camps in Hong Kong, which was still British then.

That first evening we arrived at the farm I asked Michael – he was the farm school manager at Nethercott, and, after all these years, an old friend – to be a little bit careful about how he treated Ho, to go easy on him. Michael could be blunt with the children, pointing at them, firing direct questions in a way that demanded answers. Michael understood. The truth was that everyone down there on the farm was fascinated by this silent little boy from Vietnam, mostly because they'd all heard about the suffering of the Vietnamese Boat People, but this was the first time they'd ever met one of them.

Ho had an aura of stillness about him that set him apart. Even sweeping down the parlour after milking, he would be alone and intent on the task

in hand – working methodically, seriously, never satisfied until the job was done perfectly.

He particularly loved to touch the animals, I remember that. Looking wasn't enough. He showed no fear as he eased his hand under a sitting hen to find a warm new-laid egg. He would hold a hen or a duck when no one else would. When she pecked at him he didn't mind. He just stroked her, calmed her down.

Moving the cows out after milking he showed no sign of fear, as many of the other children did. He stomped about in his wellies, clapping his hands at them, driving them on as if he'd been doing it all his life. He seemed to have an easiness around the animals, an affinity with the cows in particular, I noticed.

I could see that he was totally immersed in this new life in the country, loving every moment of every day.

The shadow that had always seemed to hang over him back at school was lifting; the frown had gone.

On the Sunday afternoon walk along the River Okement, I felt him tugging urgently at the sleeve of my coat, and saw that he was pointing. I looked up just in time to see the flashing brilliance of a kingfisher, flying straight as an arrow down the middle of the river. He and I were the only ones to see it. He so nearly smiled then. There was a new light in his eyes that I had not seen before.

He seemed so observant, so fascinated with this new world around him, and so confident around the animals, that I was beginning to wonder about his past, whether maybe he might have been a country boy back in Vietnam when he was little. He seemed more at home in the countryside of Devon than any of us city dwellers from London. I was longing to know, longing to ask him, but I dared not. I did not want to risk upsetting him. But moments later, I felt his cold hand creep into mine. That had certainly never happened before. I squeezed it gently and he squeezed back. This was every bit as good as talking,

I thought. So I asked him no questions, just smiled down at him and kept my silence.

Once a week during our visits, Michael used to come up in the evening to read one of his stories to the children. He was a writer and he liked to test his stories out. We liked listening to them too – he never seemed to get offended if any of the children nodded off. And they were so tired that they often

did. We teachers would have them all washed and ready in their dressing gowns (not easy, I can tell you, when there are nearly forty of them!). We would hand round mugs of steaming hot chocolate, and gather them round the fire in the sitting room for Michael's story.

On this particular evening, the children were noisy and all over the place, high with excitement. They were often like that when it was windy outside, and there'd been a gale blowing all day. It was a bit like rounding up cats. We thought we'd just about managed it, and were doing a final count of heads, when I noticed that Ho was missing. Had anyone seen him? No. The teachers and I searched for him all over the house. No one could find him anywhere. Long minutes passed and still no sign of Ho. I was becoming more than a little worried. It occurred to me that someone might have upset him, and that Ho had run off, just as he had a few times back at school. Out there in the dark he could all too easily get himself lost and frightened. He was in his dressing gown and slippers the last time anyone saw him, that much we had established. But it was a very cold night outside. I was trying to control my panic when Michael walked in, manuscript in hand. He looked worried.

"I need to speak to you," he was whispering to me so that others shouldn't hear. "It's Ho." My heart missed a beat. I followed him out of the room. "Listen," he said, "before I read to the children, there's something I have to show you."

"Look," he whispered. "Listen. That's Ho, isn't it?"

Ho was standing there under the light stroking Hebe's neck, and talking to her softly. He was talking! Ho was talking, but not in English – in Vietnamese, I supposed. I wanted so much to be able to understand what he was saying. As though he were reading my thoughts, he switched to English at that very moment, speaking without hesitation, the words simply flowing out of him.

"It's no good if I speak to you in Vietnamese, Hebe, is it? Because you are English. Well, I know you are really from Austria, that's what Michael told us, but everyone speaks to you in English." Ho was almost nose to nose with Hebe now. "Michael says you're twenty-five years old. What's that in human years? Fifty? Sixty? I wish you could tell me what it's like to be a horse. But you can't talk, can you? You're like me. You talk inside your head. So do I, except when I'm with you. I wish you could talk to me, because then you could tell me all about yourself, how you learned to be a riding horse. And you can pull carts too, Michael says. And you could tell me what you dream about. You could tell me everything about your life, couldn't you?

"I'm not twenty-five, Hebe. I'm only ten. But a lot has happened to me. Do you want to hear it? Your ears are twitching. I think you understand every word I'm saying, don't you? Do you know, we both begin with H, don't we? Ho. Hebe. No one else in my school is called Ho, only me. And I like that. I like to be like no one else. The other kids have a go at me sometimes, call me Ho Ho Ho because that's how Father Christmas talks. Not very funny, is it?

"Anyway, where I come from in Vietnam, we never had Father Christmas. We didn't have a horse but we had big cows, very strong, for the farm work, and ducks, many ducks. I lived in a village. My mum and dad worked in the rice fields, but then the war came and there were soldiers everywhere and aeroplanes. And there were lots of bombs falling. The houses were on fire, our house too. Many people died, my grandpa was one of them.

So then we moved to the city, to Saigon. We had to. It was not safe to stay. I hated the city. I had two little sisters. They hated the city too. No cows, no ducks, no fields. The city was so crowded. But not as crowded as the boat. I wish we had never got on that boat but my mum and dad said it would be much safer for us to leave. On the boat there were hundreds of us, and there wasn't enough food and water. There wasn't the room even to walk about, we were packed so tightly together. And there were storms too, big waves. We were wet and cold. I thought I was going to die. But it was my mum and dad and my two sisters who died. By the time we landed I was the only one in the family left.

"Then one day a big ship came along and picked us up, me and a few others. I remember someone asked me my name, and I just couldn't speak. I was too sad. That's why I haven't spoken to anyone since then – only in my head, like I said. I talk to myself in my head all the time, like you do.

"They put me in a camp in Hong Kong, which was horrible. I could not sleep, I just kept thinking of my family, all dead in the boat. I kept seeing them again and again. I couldn't help myself. I wasn't alone. There were many children like me, all wondering what would happen to us. After a long while, I was adopted by Auntie Joy and Uncle Max who came to find me in the camp. They wanted a child of their own, they said, and they chose me.

"They took me in an aeroplane to London – that's a long way from here. It's all right in London, but there are no cows or hens or ducks, or horses like you. I like it here. I want to stay here all my life. Sometimes at home, and at school, I'm so sad that I feel like running away. But with you and all the animals I don't feel sad any more."

All the time Ho was talking, I had the strangest feeling that Hebe was not only listening to every single word he said, but that she understood his sadness, and was feeling for him, as much as we did, as we stood there listening in the darkness.

Ho hadn't finished yet. "I've got to go now, Hebe," he said. "Michael's reading us a story. But I'll come back tomorrow evening, shall I? When no one else is about. *Night-night. Sleep tight. Don't let the bedbugs bite.* That's what Auntie Joy says when she switches out my light." And he stroked Hebe's neck one last time, before running into the house, almost tripping over the doorstep as he went.

Michael and I were so overwhelmed that for a minute we couldn't speak. We decided not to talk about it to anyone else. It would seem like breaking a confidence, somehow.

For the rest of the week down on the farm, Ho remained as silent and uncommunicative as before. But I noticed now that he would spend every moment he could in the stable yard with Hebe. The two had become quite inseparable.

As the coach drove off on the Friday morning, I sat down in the empty seat next to Ho. He was looking steadfastly, too steadfastly, out of the window. I could tell he was trying his best to hide his tears. I didn't really intend to say anything, and certainly not to ask him a question. It just popped out. I think I was trying to cheer him up.

"Well, Ho, didn't we have a lovely time?"

Ho didn't turn round.

"Yes, Miss," he said, soft and clear. "I had a lovely time."

During these last 40 years, Farms for City Children has welcomed over 90,000 city children and their teachers down on the farm, to our three farms in fact. They have come for their farming weeks to Nethercott House, in deepest Devon, where it all started so many years ago; to Lower Treginnis, by the sea, near St David's in Wales; and to Wick Court, near Arlingham in Gloucester, on the banks of the River Severn. Teachers have frequently said that a child can learn more in a week down on the farm than in a year in the classroom.

If, as a child, parent or teacher, you are interested in bringing your school down to one of the farms, or you would like in any way to support the charity in this work, then it would be grand to hear from you.

Please contact us at
www.farmsforcitychildren.org

Clare and Michael Morpurgo